The Garbage Bandits
and the Attack of the Trash

Written & Illustrated By Amanda Kowalsky

ISBN: 9798461810078

This book is dedicated to my love, Kat, who always believes in me. And to my kids, who love listening to my stories.

(Skates really fast)

Rocky

Sal

Petunia

(Loves to poop on cars)

(Eats lots of pizza)

Let me introduce myself. My name is Rocky, and these are my friends Sal and Petunia. I am a raccoon who loves to skate. Sal is a pigeon who loves to poop on everything, especially cars. And Petunia is a opossum who loves to eat as much pizza as she can.

We call ourselves the Garbage Bandits.

Staying up all night, eating trash, and skating fast is what we do.

We are good at finding trouble, even when we aren't trying to find it. It seems to follow us wherever we go...

...and is always lurking right around the corner.

Sometimes humans think we are the bad guys, but they just don't understand us.

We may eat trash and skate, but we also help keep the city safe at night. We are only a phone call away.

A few weeks ago, our friend Patchy called us and said
something strange was happening at the Griffin City dump.

We got down there quickly to see how we could help. The junkyard geese were hiding instead of chasing us like they usually did. That was not a good sign.

When I saw Patchy surrounded by garbage with teeth and eyes and arms, I couldn't believe my eyes. The trash had come alive, and they were ready for a fight.

And we were ready to kick some trash monster butt. Sal and
Petunia did their best, but there were too many monsters.
We needed a new plan.

I am the brains of our group, and when I saw a trash truck,
inspiration struck me like a fresh bag of yummy garbage.
We were going to go clean up the streets.

Meanwhile, somewhere top secret, an evil villain named Clarence, also known as Super Duper Bad Man, watched the chaos he had created unfold.

He would never forget when the Bandits accidentally bumped into him and made him drop his favorite banana ice cream.

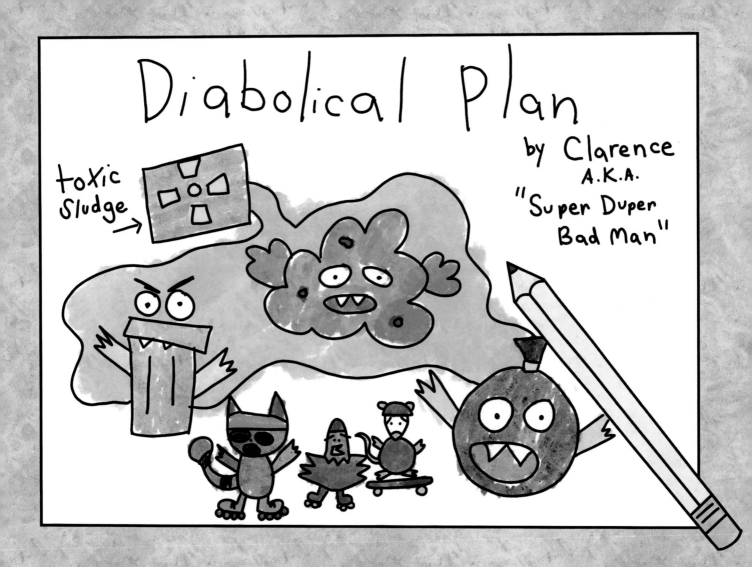

So he came up with the most diabolical plan to defeat the Garbage Bandits.

He brewed up a toxic sludge made of the grossest items he could find.

He put the toxic sludge in all the dumpsters across
Griffin City, knowing it would create stinky monsters
made of trash.

We tried our best to clean up, but it wasn't enough. We were
still outnumbered, and the monsters were wreaking havoc.

They were having a pizza party in the streets. They had made the pizza chef make them a bunch of pizzas, and they didn't even leave a tip.

They were trashing local businesses and taking selfies to show off their new bling.

They were stealing candy and money from purses so they could buy snacks. They were very naughty.

We then met a small human called Isaac, who wanted to help us take down these trash monsters.

When a monster knocked a box of laundry soap onto my head, it gave me a super awesome idea.

I got my friends together, and with the help of Isaac, we dumped a whole bunch of soap into the washing machines.

We turned the washing machines on the Super Duper Dirty setting, and it didn't take long before they created enough soap to cover the entire city.

The soap overflowed into the streets, and bubbles filled the air.
The trash started panicking.

It was working! The toxic sludge was washing off. The monsters were goners, and they knew it.

The trash monsters turned back into regular trash. The streets were messy, but the nightmare was over.

The police didn't know what to do. They couldn't arrest
the trash, and they didn't know who was responsible.

Super Duper Bad Man threw a major tantrum when he saw what had happened to his creations. But he will come up with another scheme soon enough.

We finished cleaning up the city as best as we could and returned the trash truck. We then snuck out of there while the junkyard geese weren't paying attention.

Next time Griffin City needs help, we will be there. Until then we will be skating with our friends.

We decided to take a break from the trash and eat pizza instead. We hope the pizza doesn't come alive.

Did you know?

-Raccoons have 5 fingerlike toes on each paw. They use their paws in various ways, such as scratching, swimming, climbing, digging, grabbing, and opening objects.

-Opossums are beneficial and often misunderstood. They can eat up to 5,000 ticks in a season, which helps to protect humans from Lyme disease and other dangerous diseases that ticks carry.

-Opossums are resistant to most forms of snake venom because of a protein in their blood that binds to the toxins and neutralizes them.

-Many centuries ago, pigeon poop was considered quite valuable. It was used as a fertilizer, and people often hired guards to keep people from stealing the pigeon poop from their coops.

About the Author/Illustrator

I am an artistic writer living in Cuyahoga Falls, Ohio, with my partner and best friend, Kat, and our three kids, Kira, Isaac & Griffin. Even though my main job is as an accountant, I love reading and have always wanted to write books. Ever since I was a small child, my head has been filled with stories I have made up and stories I have read. I think it is important always to follow your dreams, even when it seems difficult. My most favorite series are Harry Potter, Series of Unfortunate Events, and Goosebumps.

As a neurodiverse person, I have always had a more challenging time fitting in and making friends. Reading, writing, and my art all have helped me to find my place in the world and have helped me connect with other people. To fellow neurodiverse children, teenagers, and adults, my advice is to immerse yourself in your special interest whenever you can and share it with whoever is willing to listen.

The Garbage Bandits
Go to School

Written & Illustrated By Amanda Kowalsky